JR. GRAPHIC AMERICAN LEGENDS

DANIEL BOONE

Andrea P. Smith

PowerKiDS
press

New York

Published in 2012 by The Rosen Publishing Group, Inc.
29 East 21st Street, New York, NY 10010

First Edition

Editor: Joanne Randolph
Book Design: Planman Technologies
Illustrations: Planman Technologies

Library of Congress Cataloging-in-Publication Data

Smith, Andrea P.
 Daniel Boone / by Andrea P. Smith. — 1st ed.
    p. cm. — (Jr. graphic American legends)
 Includes index.
 ISBN 978-1-4488-5194-2 (library binding) — ISBN 978-1-4488-5226-0 (pbk.) — ISBN 978-1-4488-5227-7 (6-pack)
 1. Boone, Daniel, 1734–1820—Juvenile literature. 2. Pioneers—Kentucky—Biography—Juvenile literature. 3. Explorers—Kentucky—Biography—Juvenile literature. 4. Frontier and pioneer life—Kentucky—Juvenile literature. 5. Kentucky—Biography—Juvenile literature. 6. Kentucky—Discovery and exploration—Juvenile literature. 7. Boone, Daniel, 1734–1820—Comic books, strips, etc. 8. Frontier and pioneer life—Kentucky—Comic books, strips, etc. 9. Kentucky—Discovery and exploration—Comic books, strips, etc. 10. Graphic novels. I. Title.
 F454.B66S65 2012
 976.9'02092—dc22
 [B]
                                                    2011001714

Library of Congress Cataloging-in-Publication Data

CPSIA Compliance Information: Batch #PLS1102PK: For Further Information contact Rosen Publishing, New York, New York at 1-800-237-9932

Contents

Main Characters

Daniel Boone (1734–1820) Legendary **frontiersman**. He helped **blaze** a trail through the Cumberland Mountains. The trail became known as the Wilderness Road.

Rebecca Bryan (1740–1813) Daniel Boone's wife. She raised ten children with Boone.

John Stuart (?–1769) A **companion** on Boone's first trip through Cumberland Gap. He probably died during the trip.

John Finley (1700s) A frontiersman. He explored Kentucky along the Ohio River fourteen years before Boone.

Jemima Boone (c. 1762–1800s) Boone's daughter. She was **kidnapped** by the **Shawnee** when she was fourteen years old.

DANIEL BOONE

IN 1734, DANIEL BOONE WAS BORN IN PENNSYLVANIA. HE LEARNED TO HUNT WHEN HE WAS A YOUNG BOY.

WHERE ARE YOU OFF TO NOW, DANIEL?

I'M GOING HUNTING.

YOU SPEND ALL OF YOUR TIME IN THE **WILDERNESS**.

I JUST LOVE BEING OUT THERE, PA.

6

BOONE COULDN'T STAY PUT FOR LONG, THOUGH. SOON HE WENT EXPLORING AGAIN.

THIS KENTUCKY SURE IS FINE COUNTRY.

LEGEND SAYS THAT BOONE NEVER GOT LOST A DAY IN HIS LIFE.

LEGEND ALSO SAYS THAT ONE YEAR HE HAD TO SPEND THE WHOLE WINTER IN A CAVE.

I HOPE THIS SNOW LETS UP SOON.

IN 1769, JOHN FINLEY ASKED BOONE TO FIND A WAY THROUGH THE CUMBERLAND MOUNTAINS INTO KENTUCKY.

THERE'S SUPPOSED TO BE A **GAP** IN THE MOUNTAINS.

MAYBE IF WE FOLLOW THIS OLD INDIAN TRAIL, WE'LL FIND IT.

WE MADE IT THROUGH THE GAP.

WE'RE IN KENTUCKY!

I'VE NEVER SEEN SO MUCH GAME IN ONE PLACE BEFORE.

IT'S TRULY PARADISE HERE.

8

BOONE AND FINLEY SPENT SOME TIME HUNTING AND COLLECTING FURS.

AT LEAST WE'RE STILL ALIVE.

THEY'RE TAKING EVERYTHING, THOUGH!

AFTER NATIVE AMERICANS RAIDED THEIR CAMP, BOONE AND FINLEY PARTED WAYS.

DANIEL CONTINUED TO EXPLORE KENTUCKY. IN A FAMOUS STORY, HE HAD ANOTHER RUN-IN WITH INDIANS.

I HOPE THOSE TREES ARE SOFT!

IN 1775, A TRADING COMPANY HIRED BOONE TO CUT HIS OWN TRAIL THROUGH THE CUMBERLAND GAP.

WE NEED YOUR **TRACKING** SKILLS, DANIEL.

YOU'RE THE BEST FRONTIERSMAN AROUND.

I'D LOVE TO GIVE IT A TRY.

ALL RIGHT, MEN. STAY CLOSE AND YOU WON'T GET LOST.

THE TRAIL THAT BOONE MADE BECAME KNOWN AS THE WILDERNESS ROAD.

THE MEN BUILT A **STOCKADE** ALONG THE RIVER. SOON SETTLERS MOVED HERE. THEY NAMED THEIR NEW TOWN BOONESBOROUGH AFTER DANIEL BOONE.

JEMIMA AND THE GIRLS LEFT SIGNS ALONG THE TRAIL.

THEY'RE BREAKING THESE BRANCHES ON PURPOSE.

THE GIRLS ARE HELPING US FIND THEM.

DADDY!

I WAS SO SCARED!

YOU FOUND US!

BOONE AND THE OTHER MEN **RESCUED** THE GIRLS.

IN 1784, JOHN FILSON WROTE A BOOK ABOUT KENTUCKY. HE INCLUDED A **BIOGRAPHY** OF THE LEGENDARY FRONTIERSMAN, DANIEL BOONE.

THEN IN THE 1820S, JAMES FENIMORE COOPER WROTE ABOUT A MAN NAMED NATTY BUMPPO.

Timeline

November 2, 1734   Daniel Boone is born in Berks County, Pennsylvania.

1750   The Boone family moves to North Carolina.

August 14, 1756   Daniel Boone marries Rebecca Bryan.

1765   Daniel Boone travels to Florida with some friends to explore the area.

1767   Daniel Boone goes to Kentucky twice to hunt, trap, and explore the region.

1768   John Finley asks Daniel Boone to find a gap through the Cumberland Mountains from North Carolina and Virginia into Kentucky.

Spring 1775   Daniel Boone blazes the Wilderness Road through the Cumberland Mountains. He forms a settlement named Boonesborough along the Kentucky River.

Fall 1775   Daniel Boone moves his family from North Carolina to Boonesborough.

July 1776   Daniel Boone's daughter, Jemima Boone, is kidnapped by Shawnee warriors.

February 1778   Daniel Boone is kidnapped by the Shawnee and adopted.

October 1779   Twenty thousand pioneers settle in Boonesborough.

1784   John Filson publishes a book about Kentucky, which includes a biography of Daniel Boone.

June 1, 1792   Kentucky becomes the fifteenth state.

1799   Daniel Boone moves his family to St. Louis, Missouri.

1803   The United States buys the Louisiana territory from France in the Louisiana Purchase.

1820   Daniel Boone dies at 85 years of age.

Glossary

biography (by-AH-gruh-fee) Book that gives a history of a person's life.

blaze (BLAYZ) Make a mark on a tree or rock to show a trail.

companion (com-PAN-yun) A friend or a pal.

frontiersman (frun-TEERZ-mun) A person who lives and works in an area that has not yet been settled.

gap (GAP) A pass, or opening, through the mountains.

homey (HOM-ee) Comfortable or homelike.

kidnapped (KID-napt) Carried off a person by force.

legend (LEH-jend) A story, passed down through the years, that cannot be proved.

rescued (RES-kyood) Saved someone or something from danger.

replica (REH-plih-kuh) A copy.

restless (RES-less) Uncomfortable staying in one spot, wanting to move around.

Shawnee (shah-NEE) Native Americans who lived in the Ohio Valley, which includes Kentucky.

stockade (stah-KAYD) A wooden wall made of large, strong posts. The posts are put upright in the ground to help protect the area inside the wall.

swamp (SWOMP) A wet land with a lot of trees and bushes.

tracking (TRAK-ing) Following a trail.

wilderness (WIL-dur-nis) An area that has no lasting settlements.

Index

Web Sites

Due to the changing nature of Internet links, Power Kids Press has developed an online list of Web sites related to the subject of this book. This site is updated regularly. Please use this link to access the list:

www.powerkidslinks.com/JGAM/boone